M✳NDAY

"AAAAAAAHHHH!!!"

"ZOMBIE!!! ARE YOU OK?!!!" my mom and dad asked as they rushed in my room.

"Yeah, I'm all right. It's just. . .you forgot to leave the nightlight on."

"Aren't you old enough to go to sleep without a nightlight?" my dad asked.

"Uh. . .well, it's just that it gets **REALLY DARK**, and. . .uh. . .I'm kinda scared."

"Honey, there are no such things as monsters," my mom said. "And no matter how ugly they are, villagers are mobs too, you know."

"I know, Mom. It's just. . .it's just. . .forget it," I said, feeling too **EMBARRASSED** to talk about it.

"All right. Well, go to sleep, son," my dad said.

"Nighty-night, dear," my mom said.

Click. . .

"MOM!"

"Oh, sorry."

Clack. . .

Yeah, I know.

I'm thirteen years old, and I'm still afraid of the dark.

And I feel like a real Zombaby because I can't go to sleep without my NIGHTLIGHT. . .

And my blanky. . .

And Mr. Cuddles. . .

My stuffed Minecraft pig.

It's just that, when its dark I feel like something in the dark is going to get me.

You know. . .something like. . .

A clown. . .

Or a doll. . .

Or a **CLOWN DOLL!**

WHAT?!!!

Oh, man, I'm scaring myself.

And wetting myself.

But, you know, I don't think I'm the only kid who's scared of the dark.

I'll bet every kid at school is scared of the dark.

They just act all tough so they can look good.

You know, like Endermen.

They look all tall, dark, and courageous.

But I bet if you put them in a nice dark cave with some scary noises and some howling winds, the only things they'll be moving. . . is their **BOWELS**.

But you know what?

I think it's time that I prove to the world that I'm no longer a Zombaby.

I mean, I should be able to **MOAN AND GRUNT** in dark caves like the rest of the manly Zombies out there, right?

That's it!

I think it's time I show the world that Zack Zombie is not going to be afraid of anything!

"Prrffft."

"AAAAAAAHHHHH!!!"

"ZOMBIE!!! ARE YOU OK?!!!" my mom and dad asked as they rushed into my room.

"Mom! I heard a **STRANGE NOISE** that sounded like somebody was ripping out a duck's guts!"

"Oh, Zombie. . .it's only Wesley tooting."

Then I looked at my little brother sleeping.

Prrffft.

 TUESDAY

So our town looks totally different now.

Something tells me somebody gave the Gnomes the **WRONG PLANS** when they promised to rebuild the town.

Either that, or they wanted to move in.

I mean, like now all the houses have round doors and they have mushroom tops.

And now we have these big green sewer pipes that come out of the ground everywhere.

Now, don't get me wrong.

It's kind of nice having a **SEWER SYSTEM**.

Before, it was a real mystery where our poop went.

I mean, I asked my mom once where my poop goes when I drop it down the big hole in the backyard.

"It goes to the human world," my mom said.

"Seriously? Whoa."

Yeah, I felt really bad for humans for a long time.

I mean, I wouldn't mind sharing a bit of myself with the human world and really connecting with them.

But something tells me they probably **DON'T WANT** what I've been sharing so far.

But now, we have our own sewer system.

The funny thing is, even though now I know that my poop goes down the sewer.

Where it goes from there, nobody knows.

So I asked my mom again.

"It goes to the human world," she said.

Something tells me that my mom doesn't like humans very much.

I went to go see Steve to see if he could give me some tips on how to be BRAVE.

"Hey, Zombie! What's shakin'?"

Man, I was really hoping he wouldn't notice.

"Oh. . .I just ran into a cat before I came here," I said as I picked my butt off the floor.

"Wait. . .What?"

"Nothing, what's up with you, Steve?"

"Uh. . .nothing. . .nothing."

"Hey, I have a question for you," I said.

"Shoot."

Steve is so strange sometimes.

So I pulled out my **BOW AND ARROW** and I shot him.

"Dude! What did you do that for?"

"Uh. . ." I said as I stood there confused.

"Whatevers, man," Steve said as he took the arrow out of his nostril.

"So, what's your question?"

"Are you **AFRAID** of anything?" I asked him, a little embarrassed.

"What, you mean like monsters and stuff?"

"Yeah."

"Naw. I'm not afraid of monsters. It's the other stuff that really creeps me out."

"Really? Like what?"

"Well, I'm really afraid of swallowing my gum," Steve said with a serious look on his face.

"Seriously?"

"Yeah, they say that if you swallow your gum, you can't poop for like **SEVEN YEARS.**"

"Whoa."

Kinda makes sense, though.

It would explain what happened to my Uncle Wrigley.

He held the record for the **LONGEST TIME** without going to the bathroom.

It was really sad when he ran into that charged creeper, though.

Poor town didn't stand a chance.

Nasty. . .

"I'm really afraid of other weird stuff, too," Steve said. "Like I went to a witch doctor, and he said I have Hippopotomonstrosesquippedaliophobia."

"What's that?"

"He said it's a fear of **LONG WORDS**."

"Whoa."

"Yeah, well. . .I'm really afraid of the dark," I said. "I can't go to sleep without my nightlight."

"Seriously? How come?"

"I don't know. I feel like something is watching me and it wants to get me."

"Like what? A giant mutant spider? Or a three-headed dragon or something?"

"More like. . .a clown."

I could tell Steve was really thinking seriously about that one. He usually looks red and CONSTIPATED when he's deep in thought.

"PFFFFFFFFTTTT!" he blurted out as he fell down laughing.

"Hey, that's not funny, man," I said. "I think clowns are designed for the sole purpose of traumatizing kids."

"He. . .he. . .sigh," Steve said, catching his breath. "No seriously? Clowns?"

"Forget it, man," I said as I picked up my butt and started walking away.

"Dude, I'm sorry, I didn't mean to laugh," Steve said. "I guess we're all afraid of something."

"But I don't want to be afraid anymore. I want to be brave and strong, and **REALLY MANLY**," I said.

"Well, then you're going to have to face your fears and kick its butt!" Steve said making a kicking motion at me.

I wished he hadn't done that, though. . .

I had a really hard time finding my butt after that.

WEDNESDAY

Today, I was walking to school and I heard a really weird noise coming from one of the big green sewer pipes.

As I walked closer to it, I heard banging and talking.

Now, all the kids at school were saying that there were **ALLIGATORS** in the sewers.

I really didn't want to get my head chomped off, so I decided to walk around it.

Then, all of a sudden. . .

"Its-a me, Marco!"

"What the what?!!!!"

I got so scared, I jumped out of my skin.

No, seriously. I looked like a green version of Skelly.

"Hey there! Im-a Marco," the weird dirty little man with the **BIG MUSTACHE** and red and blue overalls said.

"Hello there," I said to the dirty old man.

"Hello, my name is-a Marco and I'm-a from the Italiano Biome. I'm-a worker of the sewer, here to keep your sewers-a nice and poopy," he said. "And this is my-a brother Loogie!"

Then another dirty little man in **GREEN AND BLUE OVERALLS** jumped out of the sewer.

"Oh yeah! Its-a me, Loogie!"

"What?!!!"

Then the other guy hacked really loud and spit in the sewer pipe.

"HHHHAAACCCK—PTTTOOOO!"

I guess these must be the guys who take care of the sewers.

"Hi, I'm Zombie. I live in this town. It's good to meet you."

"Hello, Zombie!" the one in red and blue overalls said. "Tell me, do you happen to know where-a the **SEWER FAIRY PRINCESS** is?"

"Sewer Fairy Princess?"

"Yes! Mamma mia, we search in all of the pipes looking for her, but we have notta find her."

"No, I haven't seen a sewer fairy princess," I said, thinking that these guys have been working in the sewer way too long. "But if I see her, I'll be sure to let you know."

"Okey dokey!" the green one said as he jumped back down into the sewer.

It's a good thing he did, too.

I didn't have the heart to tell him he had a wad stuck to his mustache.

The one with the red and blue overalls seemed sad. But then he went back to his business.

Man, I missed my chance, though.

I really wanted to ask those guys where my **POOP GOES**.

✻ THURSDAY ✻

BANG! BANG!

CLANK! CLANK!

Huh? Whuzzat?

BANG! BANG!

CLANK! CLANK!

I woke up early to the sound of
WEIRD NOISES coming from the
house.

When I went downstairs, my parents
were up but they looked really tired.

"What's all the noise, Mom?"

"Oh, it's the new sewer workers. They're attaching our house pipes to the sewers today, so they started early."

"Early? They started in the middle of the day when every responsible Mob is sleeping," my dad said. "Don't they know people have jobs?"

"Well, we are going to have real running water, and we are going to have a **REAL TOILET**. The brochure says that it even occasionally overflows. Isn't that wonderful?"

"Peachy," Dad said.

BANG! BANG!

CLANK! CLANK!

It was too loud to go back to bed, so I thought I would watch some TV to kill some time before school.

My favorite show is on. . .yes!

So I just hopped on the couch and watched my favorite show, Square Bob Sponge Pants.

Oh, man, I love this show.

"We interrupt this completely brainless kids show for an important announcement."

Huh?

"It seems there have been a series of Mob disappearances around town. A few missing Mob kids were last seen at the entrance

to the new town municipal sewer system. Some say they were eaten by alligators. Others say they were abducted by aliens living in the sewers. Others say they deserve what they got for playing around a creepy entrance to the city sewer system.

But If you have any information of the whereabouts of these Mob kids. . .like if you find a shoe with one of the kid's names on it written in blood—please do not go bravely in search for them in the town's sewers. Instead, call the town police department right away.

Now back to our regularly scheduled utterly senseless children's entertainment."

Whoa. That's just crazy.

I mean, like who would be crazy enough to go into those **CREEPY SEWERS**?

Well, I guess it's something I have to think about after my potty break.

So I went to go check out our new toilet.

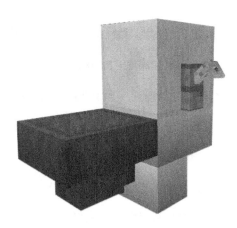

"Its-a me, Marco!"

"AAAAHHH!"

"Hello-a Zombie! How-a are you?"

"Good," I said, talking to the mustached head sticking out of the toilet.

I'm just glad he didn't come visit a few minutes later.

"Oh, yea!" The other mustached head said as it popped out of the toilet.

"HAAACCCCKKK—PTTTOOOO!" the one in the green hat said as the **YELLOW SLIME** slid down the bathroom wall.

"You haven't seen-a the Sewer Fairy Princess, have you, Zombie?"

"Sorry, guys. No sewer fairy princess in here."

"Oh, mamma mia, what are we to do-a?"

Then they both popped back down the toilet.

It's a good thing too. I was really ground-hogging it.

But I did leave them something
GREEN AND JUICY to remember
me by.

Just in case they came back.

FRIDAY

Well, today was our season field trip to Seven Flags, Great Minecraft Adventure Forrest Biome Theme Park.

It's supposed to have some of the **COOLEST RIDES**.

But the only thing I don't like about this amusement park is that it's supposed to have the

scariest haunted mansion in all the twelve Biomes.

I heard stories that this haunted mansion was so scary that the only body part you don't leave behind is your stomach.

And that's because you need it to throw up afterward.

I mean, I knew I had to face my fears, but I was definitely not ready for that.

I was just hoping that the other guys didn't want to go to the **HAUNTED MANSION**.

"Hey, guys," Skelly said. "Let's go to the haunted mansion!"

Figures.

"Yeah," Slimey said. "I heard it's so scary, it'll scare the juice out of you."

"I don't know, guys," Creepy said. "I kind of like my juice."

"Hey, I'm with Creepy," I said. "I mean, your juice should really stay in your body. You know. For health reasons."

Then I heard the noise that every middle school kid in the world DREADS, but knows so well.

"CLUCK, CLUCK, PTAW, PTAW!"

Oh boy.

"What's the matter, Zombie. . .you chicken?"

Yup. . .it was Darius.

"Zombie's a chicken! Zombie's a chicken! Zombie's a chicken!" Darius kept chanting. Then all the other kids started chanting too.

Yeah, I could've walked away. . .

And, yeah, I could've gotten a grown up. . .

And, yeah, I could've responsibly explained about my childhood **PHOBIA OF THE DARK** that stemmed from my traumatic childhood experiences. . .

But. . .

"I'm not a chicken!" I said, not sure what was coming out of my mouth.

"Watch me go through the whole haunted mansion!"

Then I looked at the guys and said, "All right, guys, **LET'S GO.**"

All of sudden, my army of pillager titans turned into toilet paper soldiers at a spitting convention.

Slimey broke into a bunch of slime bits.

Skelly's bones started to turn yellow.

And Creepy just stood there sucking on his inhaler.

"Seriously?"

Urgh! How in the world do I get myself into these things?

I think it has something to do with my mouth. It's like a broken toilet.

Or maybe it's because my brain is the size of a pea.

But all I knew was that now I had to go through the whole haunted mansion, BY MYSELF!

And, if I chickened out, I'd be knocked to last place on the SOCIAL FOOD CHAIN.

I'll end up a few pegs below humans. . .but just above Justin Bieber.

Well, I guess this is my chance to face my fears and kick its butt, like Steve said.

But why do I get the feeling it's my butt that's going to get kicked?

FRIDAY,
LATER THAT NIGHT. . .

"MOMMY, MOMMY, MOMMY, MOMMY, MOMMY!!!" I said crying as I burst out of the front door of the haunted mansion.

"HAHAHAHAHAHA!"

The big crowd that Darius gathered together outside burst out laughing.

But I didn't care. I was just glad I made it out of that **DEATH TRAP** alive.

"It's okay, Zombie. We were all scared for you," Creepy said, sucking on his inhaler.

"Yeah, you were real brave, man," Skelly said. "I don't think any of us could've stayed in there that long. Five minutes is a record."

"Yeah, Zombie. And you only lost a little of your juice," Slimey said as we turned and looked at the **GREENISH BROWN TRAIL** that led up to the haunted house.

"CLUCK! CLUCK! PTAW! PTAW!"

"HAHAHAHAHAHA!"

"Chicken! Chicken! Chicken!" all the kids kept chanting louder and louder.

Me and the guys just ran home to accept our new **POSITIONS** as the chicken boy mascots of Scaredy Catville.

Man, just when I thought I was going to face my fears and kick its butt.

Hey. . .wait a minute. . .

Where is my butt?

FRIDAY,
EVEN LATER THAT NIGHT. . .

After all the kids left the park, me and the guys went back to find. . .you know. . .my **ZOMBOOTY**.

"You must've left it in the haunted mansion," Creepy said.

"Seriously?!!!"

"Yeah, man, good luck getting that back," Skelly said. "And, you know, you don't really need a butt anyway. Look at me."

"Yeah, well, I happened to like my butt," I said. "Plus, I had my wallet and a bunch of other stuff in it too."

The other guys just looked at me with a confused look.

Man, we thought the haunted mansion was scary before, but with the park closed and the lights all out, it was seriously **TERRIFYING**.

"Hey, I really need your help, guys," I said. "I can't do this by myself."

"All right, dude," Skelly said.

"Count me in, too," Creepy said, really sucking hard on his inhaler.

"Me too, me too, me too, me too. . ." all of Slimey's bits said.

So we all crept up toward the door of the haunted mansion.

You know, this is my chance to **FACE MY FEARS** and kick its butt, I thought.

No more being afraid of the dark.

No more nightlights.

No more having to go to bed with blanky or Mr. Cuddles.

And no more being a chicken.

Yes, I'm going to be brave!

Gulp!

I just hope I live through it.

FRIDAY...
MUCH, MUCH LATER
THAT NIGHT...

Well, when we opened the door to the haunted mansion, suddenly all the lights came on.

Yeah, that's when the **BODY PARTS** really started falling off.

Now, I thought I could just walk in and find my booty just sitting in a corner somewhere.

But noooooo.

It seems that the janitor cleaned up, and he dropped it off at the Lost and Found at the end of the ride!

So, me and the guys had to go through the whole haunted mansion to get to the Lost and Found bin at the end, next to the **GIFT SHOP** and next to the vomit stalls.

So, we decided to mob up and go through with it.

Now, we made our way to the first room which wasn't so bad. . .

It was just a few creepy spiders, endermites, and silverfish.

Ha! Nothing I hadn't fought before.

But then it got weirder and creepier.

Like, the next room just had regular Minecraft Mobs walking around.

But then, all of a sudden, their faces peeled off and there were creepy human baby dolls underneath!

"AAAAAAAHHHHH!!!!"

Slimey broke apart into even smaller pieces.

Skelley lost his lunch.

And Creepy swallowed his inhaler.

As for me, well, let's just say that butts serve a purpose.

And without one, **ZOMBIE JUICE** started spraying all over the place.

Nobody left that room unsoiled.

Then we made it to a really long hallway.

We tried to walk through the room as fast as possible.

But then, suddenly, a bunch of arms came out of the wall and started **GRABBING** at us!

"AAAAAAAHHHHH!!!!"

By this time, Slimey had almost evaporated out of existence.

Skelly lost his spine. So he was just a head, torso, and legs.

And Creepy was about a few seconds from going nuclear.

Me? Well, let's just say that I think I grew eyeballs. . .on my chin.

Now, you think we'd had enough
punishment.

And you'd think that we knew when to
quit.

But noooooooooo.

We had to be **BRAVE**.

So, we made it to the last room.

It was dark, but the funny thing was
that it smelled like popcorn.

Then some lights came on, and in front
of us was a huge stage in front with
a big red curtain covering it.

Then, all of a sudden, some weird
CIRCUS MUSIC started playing. . .

And the red curtain started to open. . .

I'M GOING TO BE BRAVE.

I'm going to be brave.

I'm going to be brave.

Then, suddenly. . .

HAHAHAHAHAHAHA!!!!!

"AAAAAAAHHHHH!!!!"

Then everything went black.

SATURDAY

Okay, now I know what you're thinking.

Since I'm writing this, I made it out in **ONE PIECE**.

And you're probably thinking that I faced my fears and kicked its butt.

Well, you're wrong. . .on all counts.

For one thing, I don't think I'll be going to school for a few days.

My body doesn't move too well without a spine. . .

Or legs. . .

Or arms.

But, the good news is that I did get my butt back.

Only problem is that I have to wear it **ON MY HEAD** until they find my chin.

Makes everything smell really funny, though.

Kinda like burnt hair and garlic peanut butter.

But I can sure see better now. . .

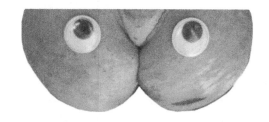

The weirdest thing was that it felt like we were being watched the whole time we were in the haunted mansion.

Later, I found out why.

It seems Darius and his goons were at the haunted mansion just waiting for us.

They were the ones who turned on the lights.

And they even **VIDEOTAPED** us as we went through the haunted mansion.

So now, we're not just scaredy cats, we're like famous scaredy cats.

Just call me Mr. Wuss Whiskerton.

So wrong. . .

☀ SUNDAY ☀

Well, now, not only do I still need a nightlight to go to sleep.

And my blanky. . .

And Mr. Cuddles.

But now everybody in the whole village knows I'm a chicken.

I think I should go to school somewhere else.

I wonder if they have school for JELLYFISH?

Steve came over when he heard what happened.

"Whoa! Dude, what happened to you?"

I couldn't hear him to well because of the **BUCKET** I was laying in.

"What?!"

"Dude! I said, what happened?!" Steve said louder.

"Oh, I'm waiting for my mom to order me some new parts."

"Seriously?"

"Yeah, I went to the haunted mansion to face my fears and kick its butt," I said. "But, as you can see, I couldn't kick much butt without any legs."

"Yeah, dude. . .you look like a jellyfish and a squid got together and had a mutant baby. . .then it vomited a pus-filled embryo sack of grossness into a bucket."

"Thanks, man. . .Sniff. . .Sniff."

"Don't worry about it, man."

"WAAAAAHHHH!!!!"

"Ah, don't cry, dude," Steve said.

"But, I'm such a **LOSER!**"

"Dude, you're not a loser. You're just sensitive, that's all."

"WAAAAAHHHH!!!!"

"You know, maybe when you get yourself back together we can go on an adventure," Steve said. "Then we'll show the world how manly you really are."

That actually sounded like a good idea.

I mean, Steve is like the bravest guy I know. So if I can do what he does, then I'll be like, seriously manly brave."

"Sounds great, Steve," I said.

Blink. . .Blink.

"Dude, but you need to put those butt chin **EYEBALLS** away. . .Those things are creepy.

Blink. . .Blink.

"And I think you might need a breath mint."

"Prffft."

M☀NDAY

I thought my recovery would take longer.

But, the Body Parts Store is using drones now to deliver packages, so it got to my house in like one day.

So awesome.

The only problem is that they were out of chins.

Yeah, so I'm going to have to wear my **BUTT CHIN** for a little while longer.

I taped my chin eyes shut so they wouldn't creep people out, though.

I taped the other hole, too, just in case I ran out of breath mints.

The good thing is that I don't have to go to school today.

Man, am I glad too.

I really didn't want to face the kids at school after Darius released that video of us at the haunted mansion.

Yeah, it's amazing how like the worst things you do go **VIRAL** in like a few minutes.

It's like the Zombie-net is like always scanning for 'Stupidity Recognition.'

I really didn't want to see the video, either.

But when Skelly and the other guys came over, we had to see it.

"Hey, Zombie. . .I see you got your new parts," Skelly said. "But. . .what's up with the tape on your chin?"

"Nothing. I just lost a **PIMPLE**, that's all."

"Whoa. That must've been a really big pimple."

Well, the good thing is that Slimey was all back together.

And Skelly got a new spine.

But Creepy was wheezing a lot. . .since he swallowed his inhaler.

"So did you guys see the **VIDEO**?" Slimey asked.

"Naw, I was too chicken. How about you?"

All the guys shook their heads.

"Well, we might as well take a look," Skelly said, pulling up a chair to my computer.

"EPIC MINERAFT MOB FAIL COMPILATION—MEET THE CHICKEN BOYS—TRY NOT TO LAUGH CHALLENGE."

Yep.

That's what it said.

Then we played it.

"URRRRGGGHH!!!"

"AAAAAAAHHHHH!!!!"

"WAAAAAHHHHH!!!!"

"MOMMY! MOMMY! MOMMY!"

"URRRRGGGHH!!!"

"AAAAAAAHHHHH!!!!"

"WAAAAAHHHHH!!!!"

"MOMMY! MOMMY! MOMMY!"

And it just repeated over and over.

"How long is this thing?"

"TEN HOURS."

"Seriously?!!"

"URRRRRGGGHH!!!"

"AAAAAAAHHHHHH!!!!"

"WAAAAAHHHH!!!!"

"MOMMY! MOMMY! MOMMY!"

So, there it was.

My whole life was going to now be defined by this one video moment.

I'm doomed.

"Hey, what's that?"

Then we saw a picture of a video that was next to it.

"BOY GETS MIRACLE TRANSPLANT—NOW HAS BUTT CHIN"

"WHAT?!!! How did they get that?!!!"

And there I was, sporting my new chin. . .looking as **MEATY** as ever.

"What the what?!!!"

At least I thought I would get some sympathy from the guys.

PFFFFFFFFFFT!

"HA, HA, HA, HA, HA!"

They just burst out laughing.

Man, so much for loyalty. . .

TUESDAY

Well, I'm back to normal today.

I had another delivery from the Body Parts store, so my chin is back to normal.

. . .And my **CABOOSE** is back to where it supposed to be.

Good thing, too. . .

It felt really weird carrying my wallet and stuff in my pockets.

As I was walking home from school today, I decided to take another route so that the other kids wouldn't see me and mess with me.

I was getting really tired of the kids asking me to **LAY AN EGG**.

I think it has something to do with my new nickname. . .

I'm going down in history as the ZOMBIE CHICKEN BOY of Minecraft.

Now, you'd think people would just forget about stuff like that.

But the last kid who got a nickname had to change Biomes.

Yeah, I felt really sorry for that kid.

I guess you can't shake a name like Bat Boy.

But then, as I was walking, I got lost.

I ended up somewhere near the entrance to the new village **SEWER SYSTEM**.

It was huge cave looking thing, and it was really dark.

And it really gave me the creeps.

Suddenly. . .

BANG! BANG!

CLANK! CLANK!

What was that?!!!

I could hear more weird noises coming from inside.

Now I was really **CREEPED OUT**, especially because the sounds started getting louder.

I could tell there was somebody or some-thing coming.

I jumped behind a tree to hide, I was so scared.

And the voices started getting louder and louder. . .and closer and closer.

I was sure they were about to get me. . .

"Mamma mia! Let'sa go-a home, eh-Loogie?"

"Okey-Dokie!"

What?

Then I came out from **BEHIND THE TREE**.

"Eh-its-a Zombie! Hello, Zombie, have you come to help us to-a find the Sewer Fairy Princess?"

"Uh. . .No. I got kinda lost, and I was wondering if you knew how to get back to my village?"

"Well, you can-a follow us through the sewer. It is a short-a cut."

"Uh. . .you mean that dark, damp, scary looking sewer over there?"

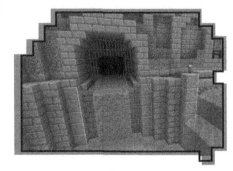

"Ya, we know-a these sewers like the back of our hands-a."

"Uh. . .No, thank you. . .I think I remember how to get home now. . .I'll see you later," I said getting the hey out of there.

Whew! That was close.

Hey, those guys might seem harmless, but going into a dark, damp creepy sewer was not something that I was ready for.

Especially not without my BLANKY. . .and Mr. Cuddles.

So, I decided to find my own way back home.

TUESDAY, LATER...

As I trekked through the forest, not really knowing where I was going, I ended up at a creepy old, beat up house in the middle of nowhere.

What the what is this **HOUSE** *doing here?*

Well, I went up to the front of the house to see if anybody was home, so I could call my mom and dad.

But after I knocked, no one answered.

So, then I walked around to the back and knocked on the back door.

Nobody answered.

Well, I guess I'm gonna have to keep walking.

But then, all of a sudden, I could swear that I saw the creepiest thing looking at me through the window.

Naw, it couldn't be. . .

I must be seeing things. . .

Then I turned around, and it was right behind me!

A **CLOWN**!

"AAAAAAAHHHHH!!!!!"

I ran and ran and ran as fast as I could.

Actually, I ran so fast, I outran the Minecraft lag.

By the time the lag caught up. . .(after about five minutes) . . .the next thing I know, I was at Steve's house.

Whew! That was close.

I knocked on Steve's door but he wasn't home, which was a **BUMMER**

I really wanted to tell him about the weird creepy clown thing I saw.

So, I just went home and told my parents about it.

But, they didn't believe me. . .

WEDNESDAY

"But it's true, Mom!

"It's true, Dad!"

"I saw a clown, and it was huge,
and it had this big forehead, and it
had **CLAWS** and these huge fangs,
and. . ."

"Zombie, I think you've been watching
too many movies," my mom said.

"Sounds like he's been playing too many
video games if you ask me," my dad said.

Urrrrrggghhh!

I got tired of trying to convince my parents of what I saw, so I just gave up and turned on the TV.

You know, maybe their right.

Maybe it was all in MY HEAD.

Clowns in sewers. . .so dumb.

"We interrupt this regularly scheduled childish program to inform you that there have been more disappearances of Minecraft Mob kids in town. Sources say that a large red-haired gentleman with a big forehead, large fangs, and floppy shoes could be involved. As well as a pair of bumbling sewer workers with big mustaches. But police have not confirmed any of this yet, so they are only ridiculous rumors.

Again, if you have any information about these missing Mobs, please do not venture into the village sewers by yourself to prove to yourself how brave you are. . .Instead, please call the local police immediately. More information at 11.

We now return you to our regularly scheduled infantile programming."

Oh, man! I knew it was real.

But what could've happened to all those kids?

You know, maybe some brave kid should venture into the sewers and see if they could rescue those kids.

But who would be brave enough. . .or stupid enough to do that?

I know!

Maybe this is **MY CHANCE** to prove how brave I really am!

Then those kids at school will stop calling me Zombie Chicken Boy of Minecraft.

All right, Zombie, you wanted an adventure, well here it is!

Bring it!

"I dare you to go down there!"

"Oh, yeah. . .well, I double dare you!"

Yup. . .you guessed it.

A bunch of kids from my school were crowding around a **SEWER PIPE** trying to dare each other to go down into the sewers.

It seems a rumor was started that there was a scary clown that lived in the sewer that eats children's souls.

Yeah, once that rumor was out, every kid in the neighborhood ran to the nearest sewer pipe to test their bravery.

. . .Or embarrass some scrawny, scared kid out of his social status.

Well, not today.

Today, I was going to be the **BRAVE** one. And I was going to prove it to the world.

"Hey, there's Zombie!"

"CLUCK! CLUCK! PTAW! PTAW!" the kids were chanting.

"Hey, Zombie! I dare you to go down this sewer pipe and stay down there for fifteen minutes," Darius yelled.

"Hey, he won't do it. He's too chicken!" one boy yelled.

"Yeah, they don't call him **ZOMBIE CHICKEN BOY** for nothing!" another boy yelled.

"HAHAHAHAHA!"

Well, it was time for me to show the world that I'm not a Chicken Boy, or a Bat boy, or a pansy, or a sissy, or a crybaby, mamma's boy, creampuff, or gutless. . .

. . .Well, gutless kinda make sense.

But, anyway, no more being the butt of everybody's jokes. . .

. . .no matter what my chin looks like.

So I grabbed my backpack and checked that I had all my **ESSENTIALS**:

- ☒ **Flashlight. Check.**
- ☒ **Booger snacks. Check.**
- ☒ **My trusty journal. Check. . . yeah, diaries are for wimps.**
- ☒ **Swiss Army pimple popper. Check.**
- ☒ **Blanky. . .**
- ☒ **. . .and Mr. Cuddles. Check!**

Hey, I need all the moral support I can get.

"Darius, I take your challenge!" I said, trying not to let my voice crack.

"WHOAAAAAAAA!" all the other kids yelled.

"And, if I survive these next fifteen minutes, then it's your turn to go down there for fifteen minutes," I said with a big grin on my face.

I could tell my **CHALLENGE** hit Darius where his heart would normally be because he was mumbling for a minute trying to get out of it.

"Uh. . .okay," he squeaked out.

So, I triumphantly climbed on top of the big green sewer pipe and looked down the eerie hole.

Maybe this wasn't a good idea, I thought as I **TIGHTLY** grabbed my backpack.

So I closed my eyes and got ready to jump.

Help me, Mr. Cuddles. . .

Then. . .I jumped.

FRIDAY

Well, it's Friday.

Now, you're probably wondering why it's Friday since I jumped down the sewer on Thursday.

Well, after Darius realized that I was going to win my dare, he made sure he didn't have to do it too.

So he and his friends **BLOCKED** the entrance to the sewer pipe so nobody could get out.

Figures.

Man, it's dark in here.

Shuffle. . .Shuffle. . .Splash. . .Splash!

What was that?!!!!

Shuffle. . .Shuffle. . .Splash. . .Splash!

Oh, man! It's the **CLOWN**! And he's gonna get me!

I tried running, but I kept running into dead ends.

Then I could hear the noises getting louder, like they were right behind me.

So I just hunkered down into a fetal position, closed my eyes and waited to get eaten.

Shuffle. . .Shuffle. . .Splash. . .Splash!

Shuffle. . .Shuffle. . .Splash. . .Splash!

SHUFFLE. . .SHUFFLE. . .SPLASH. . . SPLASH!

Oh, man, this is it!

"Its-a me, Marco!"

Wait. . .what?

"Ello Zombie, why you **POOPY** your pants-a?"

"Marco! Loogie! Am I glad to see you guys!"

"HAAACCCCKKK-PTTTOOOO! What-a are you doing here-a, Zombie?" Loogie asked me as he talked and spit at the same time.

"Well, honestly, I'm lost. Can you guys help me get back to my village?"

"Like we-a said," Marco said. "The sewers she is-a a shortcut."

"Whew! Am I so glad you guys were here."

"Well, if-a you are going to walk-a through the sewer, you will need a **UNIFORM-E**," Marco said, handing me some red and blue overalls.

"Uh. . .thanks."

So I tried them on.

They made me feel really tingly all over.

Kinda made me feel like I should be jumping down pipes and riding a go-cart.

But it would've been better in turquoise. . .and blue.

Well, after a few more hours of walking through the maze of tunnels, I started to see the **NIGHT SKY** at the end of a tunnel.

"Oh, man, am I glad to get out of here!" I said.

"Hey, maybe-a next time you can come down and-a help us find-a the Sewer Fairy Princess," Marco said.

"You bet, guys. Anytime."

And as we got closer and closer to the sewer entrance, I was feeling so much better.

SUDDENLY. . .

"RRRAAAWWRRRRR!!!"

"AAAAAAAHHHHH!!!!"

Suddenly, these gigantic orange turtle-looking monsters came out and grabbed Marco and Loogie.

"Help us, Zombie!" they yelled as the giant turtle monsters dragged them back into the tunnels.

But then. . .I **FROZE**.

I was so frozen in place, I couldn't move a muscle.

Then. . .I had to **CHOOSE**.

Should I run back and help Marco and Loogie?

Or escape through the entrance and run home where I would be nice and safe?

"Help us, Zombie!" I heard them yelling again as their voices were getting fainter and fainter.

I was so scared, I didn't know what to do.

"Help us, Zombie!"

All I could remember is how bad I felt for Marco and Loogie in the scary tunnels with those monsters. . .

. . .and how **GUILTY** I felt when I ran home to my mommy.

SATURDAY

Urgh!

How could I be such a chicken!

I left Marco and Loogie behind instead of helping them.

Those **MONSTERS** are probably eating Italian tonight, and it's all my fault!

"I'm just going to be a chicken all my life, and I'm good for nothing!" I said out loud.

"Whoa, Zombie, what's the problem, man?"

I turned and saw Steve looking at me with that confused look on his face.

I guess he's never seen a Zombie beating himself with a **SEVERED ARM** before.

"Dude! I'm a chicken, that's the problem!"

"What happened?"

"Well, there were these two sewer workers who helped me when I needed help. But when they were in trouble, I just **RAN AWAY!**"

"Seriously?"

"Yeah, man. It's because I'm such a chicken. I'm afraid of the dark, I'm afraid of monsters, and I'm even afraid of my own shadow."

"Well, your shadow is a little creepy," Steve said.

"I know what you're trying to do, man," I said. "And it's not going to work. . .I'm too **DEPRESSED.**"

"Zombie, look. No matter how painful it feels right now, it will pass," Steve said.

"Whoa. . .that's deep."

"Yeah, I saw it on an a commercial for kidney stones once."

"Wait. . .what?"

"What I'm saying is, it doesn't matter the mistake you made, what matters is that you clean it up."

"Wow, that's deep too."

"Actually, that was from a commercial for Zombie Baby Wipes."

"Huh?"

"Zombie, you just need to remember that no matter how bumpy the road, the burning will eventually go away."

"Let me guess. . .Zombie

HEMORRHOIDS?

"Yeah, how'd you know?!!"

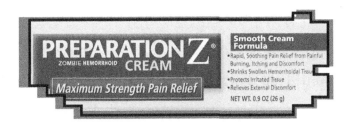

"Well, how am I supposed to fix this mistake? Those guys are probably filling some monster's **STOMACH** by now."

"Well," Steve said, "you said you wanted to come on an adventure with me, right? Well this is your chance. Let's go find your sewer buddies and the rest of the missing kids in this town."

"Seriously?"

"Yeah, I found a bloody shoe with somebody's name on it, so I think we should do this," Steve said.

Now, don't get me wrong.

I was really scared.

Not only is it really dark down there. But now I know there are giant turtle monsters.

. . .And creepy clowns.

But, this was my chance to fix a **BIG MISTAKE** I made.

A mistake I made because I chose to be a chicken instead of helping my friends.

Well, this time, I'm going to fix it.

And though I may be too late. . .and there's probably only pieces of those guys left. . .

If there's a chance they're still alive,
I'm going to help find those guys and
bring them back.

And maybe even find the lost
NEIGHBORHOOD KIDS, too.

And who knows. . .

. . .I might even find me a Sewer Fairy
Princess down there, too.

* SUNDAY *

Me and Steve walked through the tunnels for an entire day, and we still didn't find anything.

We were so tired of walking, we ended up sleeping in the sewers.

I told my mom and dad that I was having a **SLEEPOVER** at Steve's house so that they wouldn't worry.

But something tells me they're worried anyway.

Yeah, my mom really doesn't like humans.

Anyway, I'm just really glad I brought my blanky.

. . .and Mr. Cuddles.

Lick, Lick, Lick. . .

Urrrggghhhwwhuzzaatttt?

Lick, Lick, Lick. . .

"AAAAAAHHH!!! What is that?"

Me and Steve woke up to find what looked like a **BABY DINOSAUR** with a big nose, sneakers, and a long tongue licking our faces.

Actually, we found out later he was only licking the waterbugs off of our faces, which kinda made me mad.

It's not every day you get to snack on
a waterbug. . .

. . .especially the juicy fat ones.

"Hi, I'm Sushi. You want to hop on my back?" the little dinosaur said.

"Uh. . .no. I don't want to hop on your back," I said.

"You want to hop on my back?" he said again.

"No, we don't want to hop on your back. We're here to find our friends who got taken in these sewers. Have you seen two SEWER WORKERS with big mustaches in here?"

"Oh, you mean Marco and Loogie."

"Yes, Marco and Loogie. Where are they?"

"Oh no. . .They were taken to the castle. . .oh no."

Steve and I just looked at each other.

"**CASTLE?** What castle?"

"The castle where the monster lives. . .oh no." The little dinosaur said, looking sad and shaking his head.

"Well, can you take us to them?"

"Oh no. . .Whoever goes to the castle, never returns. . .oh no."

"Please, Sushi, we need to find our friends."

"Oh no. . .monster castle is no good. . .oh, no."

"Pretty please?"

"Oh no, oh no. . ."

It didn't seem like we were getting anywhere. So I gave in.

"Okay, we'll hop on your back, but only if you take us to the castle," I said.

The little guy was **SO HAPPY** that I think he totally forgot he was leading us to certain death.

Figures.

M✳NDAY

Wow, these sewers are long.

This is our second day here, and we still haven't found our friends.

But the good thing was that we didn't have to walk any more cause Sushi was like a **CAR WITH LEGS**.

Only problem was that whenever he saw a waterbug, Sushi stopped for a snack.

So it was like taking forever to get to the castle.

"I think you need a muzzle," a voice said.

Steve and I looked at each other.

"Whose there?"

"It's me. Who do you think it is?"

Steve and I looked at each other because we could swear the voice was coming out of thin air.

"Maybe he's **INVISIBLE**," Steve whispered to me.

"I can hear you, you know," the voice said. "And I'm not invisible. I'm down here."

We looked down and the weirdest looking imp was looking up at us.

He had on a big hat, he had on one eyeglass, he had a big white mustache, and he was wearing a diaper.

"Who are you?" I asked the **CREEPY LITTLE ELF**.

"My name is Frogsworth Cuddlebottom, at your service."

"Okay. . .Well, Mr. Cuddlebottom, we're in a hurry because we need to save our friends."

"You can call me Frogsworth. And, you are not going to the castle, are you?"

"Yeah, we are. So we don't have time to talk right now because we need to get there before our friends get eaten."

"Oh no. I'm sorry my boy, but if your friends were taken there, there is no hope for them."

That is not what I wanted to hear.

"You see, the castle is the home to the most fearsome, despicable and loathsome creature in all of Minecraft Sewer World. . ."

Something tells me I do not want to hear this.

"It is the home of the dastardly, Periwinkle, the **CLOWN!**"

"Seriously?!!" me and Steve both blurted.

"Yes, and Periwinkle will not just eat your friends, he will devour their souls for all eternity!"

"Seriously?!!" me and Steve both blurted again.

"I am afraid so. So, if I were you, I would turn back and go back home where you will be **NICE AND SAFE**."

Oh no. Not again.

I had a decision to make.

Do I give into my fear and run back home to my mommy?

Or do I face my fears, kick its butt, and save my friends?

But, then I remembered Steve's Zombie hemorrhoid commercial advice. . .

You know, it really left a mark on me. . .

And it left me with a **BURNING SENSATION** I couldn't shake. . .

And I felt myself swelling up with mounds of courage. . .and really itching to do something. . .

"No! I ran away before, and Marco and Loogie were taken. I am not going to run away again. . . Gulp. . .Clown or no clown!"

"Did you say Marco and Loogie? You are right! We must help them escape before the monster devours their souls!"

All of sudden, the little troll was really eager to help us.

"Why are you so eager to help Marco and Loogie all of a sudden?" Steve asked him.

"Marco and Loogie are **MY FRIENDS**. . . And, since my toilet is backed up, I am tired of smelling my own. . ."

"Whoa, T.M.I. Dude!" Steve and I said. "T.M.I.!"

Then, the little guy pulled out a muzzle out of his diaper and put it on

Sushi. Then, he tied a stick with an apple at the end to Sushi's big nose.

All of sudden, Sushi started running really fast and we were on our way.

Wow, I guess we might save our friends after all.

That is, if we're **NOT TOO LATE**. . .

TUESDAY

After traveling for another day, we finally made it to the castle.

It was a **BIG WHITE CASTLE** that look like it belonged on a cake.

It was kinda strange that a monster clown would live in that place.

"This is the monster's castle?" I asked Frogsworth.

"Oh no. This castle does not belong to Periwinkle. He took it from the princess who lived here," he said.

"You don't mean the **SEWER FAIRY PRINCESS**, do you?"

"Yes! Yes! When Periwinkle invaded her castle, she disappeared. No one has seen her since."

Me and Steve just looked at each other.

"Whoa."

Suddenly, we heard some loud noises.

BLAM!

BLAM!

BLAM!

We walked to the side of the castle and there was a giant baboon in a dress throwing **BARRELS** at the castle and yelling at the top of its lungs.

"Hoo Hoo Hoo Hoo—Ha Ha Ha Ha!"

Then when it saw us, it started throwing barrels at us!

"Run for it!"

KRESH! KRESH! KRESH!

"Madam, can you please control yourself!" Frogsworth said in a loud voice.

Then the baboon straightened up and adjusted her dress.

"What the what?"

Then Frogsworth introduced his gangly friend to me and Steve.

"Gentleman, I would like to proudly introduce you to **MISS BADONGADONK**."

"Seriously?" me and Steve said, trying not to burst out laughing.

Didn't work.

"PFFFFFFFFFTTTT!!!!"

"Hoo Hoo Hoo Hoo—Ha Ha Ha Ha!"

Then the baboon lady started throwing barrels at us again.

"RUN FOR IT!"

Kresh! Kresh! Kresh!

"Madam, please!" Frogsworth said, talking some sense into her.

After she finally calmed down, we started talking to her.

"Madam, what are you doing?" Frogsworth asked.

"I am not going to stop until I break down these walls!"

"But, madam, these walls are impenetrable. You will be here forever if you try to break them down with barrels."

"What did Periwinkle do to you, Miss Badonga. . .PFFFT. . .I mean Miss B?" Steve asked.

"Well, that clown took my **FAVORITE HAT**, and now I can't look my Sunday best without it."

We all looked at each other confused.

I think it was because her dress only covered her front, which left her huge, red, scaly backside blowing in the wind.

Nasty.

"Ooookay. Well, why don't we all work together?" I said. "We're here because Periwinkle took our friends."

Miss B. agreed, and so then we added one more soldier to our **LITTLE ARMY**.

"So how are we going to get into the castle?" I asked. "But even more important, how are we going to defeat a killer clown that eats souls?"

"I'm not afraid of him because I know his secret," Ms. B. said with a big creepy grin on her face.

"Really? Tell us! What is it?" We all asked her.

"Well, Periwinkle's power comes from **FEAR**. So, if you have absolutely no fear, then he can't even touch you."

I looked around at Steve, Frogsworth, Sushi, and Ms. B. They all seemed to be really relieved by the last thing she said.

But not me. . .

The one thing I know is that I'm so full of fear that Periwinkle is going to turn me into an all-you-can-eat **ZOMBUFFET**.

Oh, man, I'm so doomed.

WEDNESDAY

So, today's the day we storm the castle.

We really didn't know how to get into that place because it was shut up really tight.

But Steve had an **IDEA** that everybody thought could really work.

It's kind of embarrassing, though.

It involves a catapult and a crash test dummy. . .I mean zombie.

"Ready, Zombie? Okay, pull!"

"Urrrrgggggghhhhh!"

I don't think Zombies were designed
for flying through the air.

We're not AERODYNAMICALLY
designed.

I think it has to do with all of our
limbs flapping all over the place.

Or the juice trail we make through the
air.

SPLATTT!!!

Hey, it had to come down sometime.

Anyway, I made it in and I opened the
big front gate.

All the guys stormed in, but the funny thing was there were **NO GUARDS** in front of the castle.

We just walked right in.

"Hey, my ears are tingling," Steve said.

Whoa. . .Steve has ears?!!

"Something tells me it's a **TRAP**," Steve said.

"Really? What gave it away?" I heard a growly voice say.

Suddenly, six giant orange turtles rushed at us.

"AAAAAAHHH!!!!"

They captured everybody. Except me and Sushi got away.

Being covered in Zombie juice made me really **SLIPPERY** and hard to catch, especially after Sushi licked most of it off of me.

But all the other guys were captured.

"Oh no. . ." Sushi said. "They are going to the dungeon. . .oh no. Oh no."

"Sushi, do you know where the dungeon is?"

"Yes, I know where the dungeon is. . .oh no. The dungeon is where the monster keeps his dinner. . .oh no."

I would be lying if I told you that I wasn't scared. And I seriously wanted to go home.

"Take me there, buddy," I said, jumping on Sushi's back.

Then me and Sushi snuck down into the **DUNGEON** to see if we could get our friends back.

Hopefully.

I was kind of wondering how Sushi knew his way so well around the castle.

And how he was able to get away from the turtles so easily.

But then, I **FOUND OUT**.

"RAWRRRRR, Sushi, good job. Bring the other one here and throw him in the cage, RAWRRRR," the giant turtle said.

Next thing I knew, I found myself in a cell with all the other guys.

Then the giant turtle jumped on Sushi, and they rode away.

Figures.

"What gives? Sushi is with those guys?" Steve asked.

"Well, they are bred to serve their masters," Frogsworth said. "And baby dinosaurs are simple creatures that have SERVED the giant turtles for ages."

"Great, I wish you had told us that earlier," I said.

"Whose-a there?" a voice said, coming from another cell.

"Wait? Marco, is that you?"

"Mamma mia, its-a Zombie! Loogie, Zombie is-a here to-a rescue us."

"Oh yea!" I heard Loogie say.

"Well, Marco, I think we all need **RESCUING**."

"Hey, whose there?" another voice from another cell said.

"I'm Zombie," I said.
"Who are you?"

"I'm Thomas, the Enderman," the voice said. "And there's Conner, Tanner, Wyatt, and Priscilla with me too."

"You guys must be the missing kids, right?" I asked them.

"Yeah, we all got taken while we were all daring each other to go into the sewer."

So we found everybody. The only one still missing was the Sewer Fairy Princess.

"So how are we going to get out of here?" Thomas asked. "They put some **MAGIC SPELLS** on these cells, so I can't teleport out."

"I don't know, man," I said, "but hold tight. We'll think of something."

Who was I kidding, I had nothing.

And looking at the rest of my little team, I could tell they didn't have anything either.

Something tells me were going to be here for a **LONG TIME**.

At least it's better than being in the other place, getting my soul sucked out. . .Yikes!

☀ THURSDAY ☀

We were woken up by the giant turtle guards opening the doors and taking one of the **PRISONERS**.

"No, don't take her! Take me instead!" I heard Thomas say.

From where I was standing, I saw them take the girl Priscilla away to who knows where.

"Where are they taking her?" I asked Frogsworth.

"They are taking her to see Periwinkle," he said with a terrified look on his face.

"Man, I wish I could do something!" Steve yelled as he pounded the wall with his fist.

Then, suddenly, we heard some **SHUFFLING** coming our way.

"Oh no, they're coming back for another one!" Frogsworth yelled.

So, we all got in our battle-ready positions.

But instead of a guard. . .It was Sushi!

"Sushi, buddy, you came back!" I said.

"Do you want to hop on my back?" Sushi said with an innocent look on his face.

"Boy do I! Hey, help us get out of here, and I'll hop on your back forever."

Then Sushi turned around and gave the cell a really **HARD KICK** with his back legs.

Kresh!

The cage door flew open, and we all got free. Then we went and freed all the other guys.

"Hey, Thomas, do you think you can teleport everybody out of here?" I asked.

"Not all at once, but I can take you guys one at a time," he said. "But who's going to save Priscilla? I know we just met her, but she's one of us now."

"We'll take care of her," Steve said. "You just get everybody out of here."

Then Thomas started **TELEPORTING** all the kids out one at a time.

BAMF!

Me and Steve looked at each other, and we both knew what we needed to do.

Then Frogsworth and Miss B. jumped in.

"Hey, you're not going anywhere without us," Miss B. said.

Wow. . .she must really want that hat back, real bad. I guess it makes sense. She is kind of mugly.

"Right-o lads! It's time we showed this clown we are not going to put up with anymore tomfoolery," Frogsworth said.

"Huh?"

Then Marco and Loogie jumped in.

"We are here to **FIGHT-A** with you, Zombie!" Marco said.

"Oh, yeah! It's Loogie time! HAAACCKK—PTTTOOOOO!"

Then we all jumped on Sushi's back and we rode off to meet. . .

Gulp. . .

The Killer clown.

THURSDAY, ✳
✳ LATER THAT NIGHT. . .

We climbed the stairs until we made it to a huge door.

"Oh no. . .this is the room with the monster. . .oh no," Sushi said.

"Guys, remember what Miss B. said. He can't hurt us if we're not afraid," Steve whispered.

I put on the **BRAVEST** face I could put on.

But who was I kidding. . .I was toast.

Then we all opened the giant door.

Inside, there was the girl Priscilla, strapped to a huge altar at the end of the room.

And in front of her was the creepiest, ugliest, scariest clown you ever saw, with a **FLOWERY HAT** on.

He had sharp teeth and claws and everything.

Why did it have to be a clown? Why?

"Mamma mia! It is the Sewer Fairy Princess!" Marco yelled.

"Seriously?!!!" everybody said,

surprised that Priscilla was the missing princess.

"Yes, but we are-a too late. . .The monster is going to eat her-a soul!"

"Not if I have something to do with it," Miss B. said.

"Hoo Hoo Hoo Hoo—Ha Ha Ha Ha!"

Miss B. ran toward the clown with her **RED HINEY** flashing us from out of her dress.

"Ooooooh, that's going to leave a scar on my brain," Steve said.

"Hoo Hoo Hoo Hoo—Ha Ha Ha Ha!"

Miss B. cried as she was about to reach the killer clown.

Suddenly, the clown turned around and looked at her.

Next thing we know, he pulled out a bunch of **BANANAS** from out of his clown suit.

"Hoo Hoo Hoo Hoo—Ha Ha Ha Ha!"

Then Miss B. just followed the bananas into a cage and got locked in by the giant turtles.

"Well, so much for trying to take the gorilla out of the girl. . ." Frogsworth said.

"So, I guess it's going to be up to us then," Steve said as he looked at me and then looked at all the other guys.

Then everybody nodded.

"Let's do this!"

"Heeeeeyyyaaaahhhh!!!!"

Then, everybody rushed the **KILLER CLOWN**.

Well. . .

Almost everybody.

What in the world am I doing? I thought to myself as I stayed behind and hid in a corner with Sushi.

Well, you can't go up against a clown! They are like the creepiest, scariest, ugliest, monsters ever! I said to myself.

But my friends need me! I can't chicken out now!

Well, it doesn't matter, the other guys will take care of him. I'll just stay right here for backup.

Then I looked over at Sushi, and I saw a **SMALL TEAR** fall from his eye.

"What's the matter Sushi?" I asked him.

"Oh no. . .The monster is going to eat your friends. . .Oh no. . ."

"AAAAHHHH!!!!!" I heard the guys start yelling in pain.

I poked my head out of the corner, and I saw that the guys finally made it to

Periwinkle. But he had his claw hand out, and it looked like some magic was pouring out of his claw so that they were stopped in their tracks.

"Oh no. . .the monster is going to eat your friend's souls. . .Oh no. . ." Sushi said.

"AAAAHHHH!!!!!" The guys started **YELLING** in pain again.

Oh, man, what was I going to do?

Maybe I should go home and get help, I thought.

Urgh! But Mom and Dad won't believe me.

Maybe Steve can break free, I thought.

But then I heard Steve yell out in pain, "ZOMBIE! HELP US!"

All a sudden, something came over me.

I don't know what it was.

It felt like I got struck with a bolt of lightning.

But suddenly, my **PEA BRAIN** started formulating a plan.

I wasn't sure if it was going to work, especially against a killer clown that could control people's souls.

But I didn't care. I was going to help my friends, even if I was going to get eaten trying.

Whoa, this is what courage must feel like, I thought.

Then, I looked over at Sushi and he looked back.

And we both nodded in **AGREEMENT**.

Then I jumped on Sushi's back and we charged full force toward the ugly, killer clown that had my friends.

Well, here goes nothing!

"Heeeeeyyyyaaaahhhh!!!!"

THURSDAY,
EVEN LATER THAT NIGHT. . .

It's like everything was in slow motion.

I felt myself feeling more and more powerful as I **GALLOPED** closer and closer to my destiny on my faithful steed Sushi.

But his spell is going to stop you! I heard a voice inside my head say.

You can't stop his magic, it's too powerful! I heard another voice say.

He's going to eat your soul! another voice said

He's a clown, you dummy! I heard a really loud voice in my head say.

But, I didn't care.

Was I going to die? Probably.

But it didn't matter because **MY FRIENDS** needed me.

So, as I got closer and closer. . .and the gigantic, ugly, fang-faced killer clown pulled out his claw hand. . .

I heard a tiny voice in my head that sounded like Steve. And it said. . .

"IT'S TIME TO FACE YOUR FEAR AND KICK ITS BUTT!"

"Heeeeeyyyyaaaahhhh!!!!"

I jumped off Sushi and flew through the air at the killer clown.

Periwinkle lifted his claw hand and blasted me **FULL FORCE** with his magic powers.

This is it!

ZZZZZAAAAPPPP!

But, suddenly, I continued flying through the air.

For some reason, I wasn't affected by Periwinkle's powers!

This ugly clown is going down!

"Heeeeeyyyyaaaahhhh!!!!"

BOOOOOOOMMM!

My big head landed full force into the killer clown.

Periwinkle flew about twenty feet away from everybody and released his soul-crushing grip from my friend's souls.

"This cannot be!" I heard Periwinkle **SQUEAL** as his voice cracked.

Then he got up and looked at me. . .

Oh, man, I think he's really mad now.

But then, all of a sudden, he tried to run away!

This is your chance, Zombie!

I ran at him with all my might and I jumped into the air (again in slow motion) . . .and I did a super fly, mega ultra-kick motion in the air.

"Heeeeeyyyaaaahhhh!!!!"

BOOOOOOMMM!!!!

And it landed right on Periwinkle's butt cheeks.

OWOWOWOWOW!!!! Periwinkle yelled as he **HOPPED AROUND** like a frog in a hot tub.

Then all of us gathered around him.

"RAWWRRRRR!!! UGGHHH!!! MULLLNNNRR!!!"

He tried to scare us with his creepy clown face gestures, but nobody was afraid anymore.

"I'll get you for this!" he yelled as he started to shrink before our eyes.

"You'll see! I'll be back to get my revenge!" he squealed.

But he kept shrinking and shrinking until he totally **DISAPPEARED.**

"Mamma mia! We did it!" Marco and Loogie yelled. "We are number one!"

"Dude! How did you do that?" Steve asked. "How come Periwinkle's spell didn't work on you?"

"I don't know," I said. "Maybe it's because I'm awesome."

"Actually, Zombie," Frogsworth said, "it's because Periwinkle's only has power over a person's soul. And since you're a Zombie. . .well. . ."

"What. . .Seriously?!!!"

Then we released the Sewer Fairy Princess, and she gave Marco and Loogie a **KISS.**

Blech!

Then we let Miss B. out of her cage and gave her the stolen hat.

Didn't help, though. She was still butt-ugly.

And then we got Frogsworth a fresh diaper.

As for me and Steve, we just looked at each other and decided it was time to get out of this crazy place and back to our normal lives in the Minecraft Overworld.

SATURDAY

Well, we made it back home today, safe and sound.

Though, I think I will be forever **TRAUMATIZED** by the things we saw.

I'm just glad we got Miss B. a new pantsuit to go with her new hat.

Nasty.

I heard Marco and the Sewer Fairy Princess are getting married.

And Loogie is the best man.

They invited me and Steve to go to the wedding.

But we decided not to go when we heard there was a **FLYING PIRATE SHIP** circling the castle.

The entire experience encouraged Frogsworth to give up his diaper and put on his big boy pants.

I'm not sure that was a good idea, though.

Because Marco and Loogie never got around to fixing his toilet.

As for me, well, I finally know what it feels like to **FACE** my fears and kick its butt.

Funny thing was that I had the courage the entire time.

I just had to tap into it.

And all it took was my friends being in trouble, a little dragon named

Sushi, and a Zombie hemorrhoid cream commercial to do it.

It just makes me swell with pride just thinking about it.

Anyway, now that I am brave, I have a feeling that Steve is going to ask me to go on even more crazy adventures.

Like, I heard he just finished building a **TIME TRAVEL PORTAL**.

I know, crazy right.

Steve has a really big imagination sometimes.

It's a good thing that it's probably not real.

. . .Or is it?

FIND OUT WHAT HAPPENS NEXT!

ZOMBIE'S EXCELLENT ADVENTURE

Minecraft has gone through **another major update** and half of the **Minecraft Overworld has disappeared**! The only way for Zombie and Steve to figure out what happened is to **TRAVEL BACK IN TIME**.

Will Zombie and Steve be able to save their friends, and bring Minecraft back to being the **kid friendly** game loved all over the world? And what's the deal with the **EVIL CORPORATION**?